USBORNE RHYMING STORIES

PIRATE McGREW
AND HIS
NAUTICAL CREW

Written by Philip Hawthorn
Illustrated by Kim Blundell
Designed by Non Figg
Additional designs by Andy Griffin
Edited by Jenny Tyler

There's stolen treasure in this book
An old blue parrot's got it.
Gold coins she took, so take a look
And see if you can spot it.

Each page has one or two or three,
Some twenty-one in all.
So seek and see and it'll be
A perfect pirate haul.
                    Ha-Harr!

For Zak

In bygone times, in times gone by,
When life at sea was tough,
The ships had masts that spiked the sky,
With sails and ropes and stuff.

And in the taverns tales were told,
Of skull and crossbone raids,
Of plundered treasure, jewels and gold,
And other escapades.

But best of all the yarns you'd hear,
I tell you now it's true,
Was of a sea-dog buccaneer,
A pirate called McGrew.

He'd cry, "Ha-Harr!" But even though
He seemed so mad and mean,
He was, you know, as pirates go,
The worst the world had seen.

But then, one day, his luck changed tack,
And went from glum to glory.
So pin your ear-'oles firmly back,
And I'll begin my story...

Ha-Harr! For the west wind,
And tall tales so true
Of Pirate McGrew
And his nautical crew.

One night McGrew lay wide awake,
And thought about his past.
"I've never had a single break,
Nor one success - oh, blast!"

McGrew was four foot two in size,
His brain was rather slow.
He'd no peg leg and two good eyes,
But wore a patch for show.

His scraggy beard was almost grey,
His parrot had been blue.
But she had flown away one day
With Jock the cockatoo.

So now upon his shoulder sat
A tatty old canary,
Quite fat, a hat, a creased cravat,
And known as Mr. Scary.

Now each of these sad facts was known,
From England to Australia.
And so for years he'd sailed alone,
A clueless, crewless failure.

So sadly 'round his ship he paced,
The "Pardon Me" by name.
(A strange name, true, so with all haste,
I'll quickly now explain:

The queen'd had bad wind, you see,
And said, as she was launching it:
"I name this ship - Burp! - Pardon Me!
Oh dear, how most unfortunate.")

But then, just as the morning sun,
Bright gold, began to rise,
It dawned on him what must be done,
"Ha-Harr! I'll advertise!"

He scrawled, AHOY THERE! PIRATES ALL!
McGREW NEEDS YOU TO CREW!
He nailed the poster to a wall,
And said, "There, that'll do."

For weeks he didn't hear a thing,
His mood grew gloomy fast.
Then 'Ding!' the doorbell gave a ring,
"At last!" he cried, "At last!"

5

Outside he saw a tatty group,
One boomed, "Kind Sir! Good Day!
May I present my acting troupe,
We've come about your play."

McGrew looked blank, the man then went,
"Oh come! You must recall!
You wrote this fine advertisement,
AHOY THERE! PIRATES ALL!"

AHOY THERE!
PIRATES ALL!
MCGREW
NEEDS YOU
TO CREW!

McGrew thought, "Fool! He gets it wrong,
My poster's not for drama.
But wait! Ah-harr! I'll play along,
And trick the silly nana.

"'Cause once I gets 'em out to sea,
They'll all be in my power."
And so he said, "Ye'll do for me.
We sails in half an hour."

The actor bowed, "Oh, what a thrill!
So now, for your production,
Each actor will, with finest skill,
Perform their introduction."

"Oh, daar-ling! I'm Fenella Farr,
The famous drama dame.
From near to far, I'm such a star,
They toast me in champagne."

"I'm Teddy Tagg, I'm fond of food,
I play the comic roles.
I tell good jokes (they're sometimes rude)
Here's one about two moles..."
("Oh, not now Ted," the others said.)

"Hello, my name is Liz Treloar,
I'm good at all things practical.
I sew and saw and what is more,
I'm also dead theatrical."

"For years I've led this Merrie Band,
I am Sir Dick DeVyne.
I've starred in each performance, and
Remembered every word...er...line."

*Ha-Harr! For the actors
If only they knew,
For Pirate McGrew
They were now his new crew.*

Chapter Two: McGrew tells the crew his plan. They don't like it...

Sir Dick looked 'round, "I like this venue,
We'll take a nap, then dine.
Do call us when you send the menu,
'Bout nine will do us fine."

"No fear!" McGrew said, "When we feeds
  It's you who cooks for me!
    You windy wet-legged wimpy weeds,
      I gives the orders, see?"

The crew moaned, "That's a bit extreme."
Their captain laughed, "Who cares!
I have a dream, a master scheme
  To make us millionaires!

  "King Bill the Brill set sail last week,
  A ruby on his boat.
  A rare antique from Mozambique,
    And big as half a goat."

  Then Liz said, "Steal from Good King Bill?
  But he's our royal hero.
  Your chance of help is less than nil,
    It's even less than zero."

McGrew just yelled, "Heave Ho! Avast!
Weigh anchor! Slip that knot!
Now splice the mainbrace! Rig the mast!"
The actors said, "You what?"

McGrew looked cross and pursed his lips,
He'd realized suddenly,
That when it came to sailing ships,
His crew was all at sea.

And so he had to tell them how
They'd really have to learn.
"The pointy front bit's called the bow,
The back end's called the stern.

"And port is left, and starboard's right,
The crow's nest's for the look out.
And...Oh! What's this part? Hold on tight,
I'll have to get me book out."

"A bedtime story?" Teddy cried.
"Oh great!" the others said.
McGrew said nothing, simply sighed,
And tucked them into bed.

And so with hope and tug of rope
They launched their pirate trip.
Then one day through his telescope,
McGrew espied a ship.

"Ahoy there! Pirates all!" he bawled,
The crew hoorayed, "The Play!"
"Not that!" McGrew said, quite appalled.
"We raids 'em straightaway!"

Sir Dick said, "Fight with sword and gun?"
McGrew's reply was quick,
"No, no! I've only got the one,
You'll have to use a stick."

Then Ted said, "Fighting's dangerous."
"And noisy," said Miss Farr.
McGrew growled, "Rubbish! Stop this fuss!
All ready? Good! Ha-Harr!"

They leaped on board the royal boat,
With piercing pirate yells -
Like, "Death or glory!", "Slit that throat!"
And, "Last one back here smells!"

But soon they stopped in mid "Ya-hoo",
They'd noticed something weird,
The king, the crew, the ruby too,
Had strangely disappeared.

Liz found a note and held it high,
McGrew said, "Give it 'ere!
It says, 'The king's been kidnapped by...'"
Then stopped, eyes wide with fear.

"A guessing game!" said Ted, "Oh yeah!
Now, are you well acquainted?"
McGrew just whimpered "Mad Pierre..."
Then rolled his eyes and fainted.

He woke and spoke of Mad Pierre,
"He's lean, unclean and mean.
He blows his nose on people's hair,
Which makes it turn all green."

"Across each ocean, down each coast,
He's plundered, robbed and killed,
For lunch he's fond of squid on toast,
And seagull droppings - grilled.

"He has an island fiercely guarded
By all his nasty men.
Get near it and you'll be bombarded -
Ker-smash! Glug! Glug! Amen."

McGrew then sighed from deep inside,
A worn-out, weary moan.
"Oh well," he said, "at least we tried.
I give up - let's go home."

But Liz yelled, "No! They've nabbed King Bill!"
"To battle, scurvy swabs!
Let's make 'em shake and shiver, till
They look like jelly blobs."

McGrew knew what he had to do,
Once more he cried, "Set sail!"
He felt, encouraged by his crew,
Determined not to fail.

They saw such sights, both day and night,
As sailors shouldn't miss.
And all the while, for sheer delight,
Sung sea-songs such as this...

Sail! Sail! Sail the boat,
O'er the seven seas.
Swab the deck! Pull the rope!
Isn't life a breeze.

Blow! Blow! Bumpy ride,
Feeling rather sick.
Up! Down! Side to side,
Fetch a bucket, quick!

Look! Look! There's a whale,
Fountain from its head.
I spy a pirate sail!
Island straight ahead.

Sail! Sail! Such a joy...
What?
Pirate island?
LAND AHOY!!!!

Ha-Harr! For they knew
What they all had to do!
That Pirate McGrew
And his nautical crew.

Chapter Three: Liz has a great idea...sort of...

Dick roared, "The lair of Mad Pierre!
Across the sea it sits,
But how to get from here to there,
Without being blown to pieces...er, bits."

"Disguise the boat!" Liz beamed a smile,
"With green and yellow paint.
We'll look just like a desert isle,
When all the while we ain't!"

They made the topsails palm-tree green,
The deck like golden sand,
Then sailed up close without being seen,
And reached the beachy land.

They all got ready, tension rose,
It couldn't get much higher.
But as McGrew said, "Off we goes!"
Pierre's voice bellowed, "FIRE!!"

Then came a hail of cannonballs,
With vicious, nasty meanness.
Amid the frantic frets and calls,
Ted said, "I think they've seen us."

The masts went CRACK! The sails went RIP!
The splinters flew like darts.
And as McGrew turned 'round his ship,
It broke in several parts.

Again McGrew was so upset,
"I needs a new career."
But Liz said, "No! Don't give up yet,
I've got a great idea..."

"Now this is what we need to do,
First, take them by surprise.
And second, make them think our crew
Is more than four in size."

She then explained her brave intentions,
And everyone took note,
"We'll make two fabby new inventions,
From broken bits of boat."

So under Liz's expert eye,
They banged and bashed and things,
And built a boat designed to fly
By means of two great wings.

Liz made an underwater craft,
A sausage-shaped machine.
"It may look daft, but this," she laughed,
"Is called a submarine.

"Now Ted and I will go in here,
And you three fly in there."
She then explained, to make it clear,
"Attack by sea and air."

The crew exchanged supportive words,
Blew kisses, wished best wishes,
McGrew then soared toward the birds,
And Liz toward the fishes.

Ha-Harr! Ballyhoo!
And a hullabaloo,
For Pirate McGrew
And his nautical crew.

The ocean bed was gloominous,
So dingy, dark and damp,
Each fish, from shark to octopus,
Was forced to use a lamp.

Inside a stinky, slimy cave,
A door came into view.
"Let's go!" said Liz, "We must be brave."
Ted said, "Right...after you."

But at that moment both were grasped,
And bundled to the ground,
And soon a wicked French voice rasped,
"Now, what iz zees ah've found?"

Pierre then glared, "Ah'll pull your hair,
And then ah'll rip your shirts.
Ah'll pinch and punch you everywhere,
Until it really hurts."

But Ted said, "Shame, oh please don't maim us,
We've got a play to share,
It's called 'True Stories Of The Famous.
Part Seven: Mad Pierre'."

Pierre said, "Really? Right you men,
Release them to prepare.
We'll see zis drama in my den,
I bags the comfy chair."

The play told tales of blood and gore,
Of pillaging and pain.
And how Pierre won tug o'war
Against a team from Spain.

They also crooned romantic tunes,
All dreamy and ornate,
About being strewn with gold doubloons,
And kissing girls till late.

Then Ted spun yarns of men from Mars,
The audience sat wide-eyed.
And gasped with *aah*s and *oh la la*s
But then the look-out cried...

"PIERRE! PIERRE! IT'S IN THE AIR!"
The gang ran, quick as light,
And looked to where the man's wild stare
Revealed an awesome sight.

19

Above, the flying vessel loomed,
A menace in the sky.
Pierre screamed, "Men from Mars! We're doomed!
Ah'm far too young to die!"

Then Dick, McGrew, Fenella too,
Threw rotten eggs on skewers,
Which made Pierre and all his crew
Smell worse than pooey sewers.

Then green and yellow paint rained down,
Which made Pierre complain,
"We look like birds from Parrot Town,
And paint is sure to stain."

Then screaming madly, Liz and Ted,
With whips of sticks and string,
Soon bashed and beat them till they bled,
For king-napping their king.

Then Mad Pierre got out of there,
Fast followed by his men.
They sailed away to who-knows-where,
And ain't been seen again.

The airship landed, then McGrew
Congratulated Liz,
And said, "There's one thing left to do,
We all know what that is!"

The crew cheered, "Save King Bill the Brill!"
McGrew had forty fits.
"No, no! To get our biggest thrill,
We steals the ruby, twits."

Sir Dick coughed, "We'll do no such thing,
For one important reason:
To steal a jewel from the king,
Is tantamount to robbery...er...treason."

McGrew smiled sweetly, "In a way,
It's you I has to thank."
Then barked, "But if you don't obey,
I'LL MAKE YOU WALK THE PLANK!"

They searched Pierre's old bamboo huts,
But all they saw in there,
Were fishes' guts, old coconuts,
And dirty underwear.

But then they heard a muffled sound,
Inside a big, blue box.
They looked and found the king, all bound,
And wearing just his socks.

With speed they freed his majesty,
Who calmly said, "McGrew!
You've given me my liberty,
Now what can I give you?"

Then overawed beyond belief,
McGrew said, "Don't be silly!
Now here's my thermal handkerchief
In case your bottom's chilly.

"We'll find your sailors right away,
The island's pretty small.
And then my crew will do their play,
AHOY THERE! PIRATES ALL!"

Sir Dick boomed, "Friends! I'll set the scene:
The sea...a ship...full sail,
The goodies brave, the baddies mean.
Sit back and hear our story...er, tale."

Then Liz did her Pierre impression,
And spoke just like he spoke.
And Ted to finish off his session,
Said, "Now here's a brilliant joke."

Fenella then performed a speech,
And moved them all to tears.
She then sang, "Battle On The Beach"
Which brought three hearty cheers.

The king then rose and yelled, 'bravos'
With pure and perfect pleasure.
"I think, you know, your super show's
A true dramatic treasure!"

"And now, your highness," said McGrew,
"If you would go and pack,
We'll cook for you a barbecue,
And then we'll fly you back."

The king then built them, instantly,
A stage both great and grand.
And very soon they came to be
Renowned throughout the land.

McGrew gave up his pirate ways,
He'd learned a thing or two.
And wrote the most amazing plays,
Which then his crew would do.

And then the company achieved
The greatest of rewards.
One night, in tears, they all received
Academy awards.

From that night on McGrew appeared,
And introduced each play.
While all the audience clapped and cheered,
He'd clear his throat and say...

"Ha-Harr! We'll perform
An adventure for you.
'Bout Pirate McGrew
And his nautical crew..."

First published in 1995 by Usborne Publishing Ltd, Usborne House, 83-85 Saffron Hill, London EC1N 8RT, England. Text copyright © 1995 Philip Hawthorn. Pictures copyright © 1995 Usborne Publishing. The name Usborne and the device ⚑ are Trade Marks of Usborne Publishing Ltd. All rights reserved. No part of this publication may be reproduced, stored in a retrieval system or transmitted by any form or by any means, electronic, mechanical, photocopy, recording or otherwise, without the prior permission of the publisher. First published in America in August 1995. Universal edition. Printed in Portugal.